Daisy's Taxi

by RUTH YOUNG · illustrated by MARCIA SEWALL

ORCHARD BOOKS   New York

ORCHARD BOOKS   A division of Franklin Watts, Inc.
387 Park Avenue South   New York, NY 10016

Manufactured in the United States of America
Printed by General Offset Company, Inc.   Bound by Horowitz/Rae
Book design by Alice Lee Groton

10 9 8 7 6 5 4 3 2 1

The text of this book is set in 22 point Kennerly.
The illustrations are gouache reproduced in full color.

Library of Congress Cataloging-in-Publication Data

Young, Ruth, date.
    Daisy's taxi / by Ruth Young ; illustrated by Marcia Sewall.
        p.   cm.
    Summary: Daisy ferries to and from the island all day in her water taxi.
    ISBN 0-531-05921-9 ISBN 0-531-08521-X (lib.)   [1. Boats and boating—Fiction.]
I. Sewall, Marcia, ill.   II. Title.
PZ7.Y877Dai 1991   [E]—dc20   90-7735 CIP AC

To Mitchell Rose,
"simply messing...messing—about—in—boats."
R.Y.

To my favorite patch of earth, sea, and sky.
M.S.

Daisy and her rowboat are always on the water.
She rows her water taxi from the mainland to the island.

Sunup to sunset, stormy or calm,
Daisy rows out
and back.

Carrying passengers....
Big ones—Mr. Oscar Butterworth.
Small ones—Miss Amanda Wing.

Carrying packages....
Large ones—a potted palm for Mrs. West,

or a giant stuffed bear
for the Smith's new baby Wilma.

Itty bitty ones—a pair of guppies for Harold Greene.

Carrying tall things,
And very, very small things,
out and back, out and back.

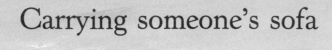

Carrying someone's sofa

or someone else's uncle.

Surprises, improvements, old friends, new babies.

All day long Daisy rows her water taxi
Out to the island, back to the mainland.

And evenings after dinner
When Harry asks,
"What would you like to do tonight, Daisy?"

Daisy says, "Take me for a row, dear."
And off they go.